Hoppy Hanukkah!

Linda Glaser   Illustrated by **Daniel Howarth**

Albert Whitman & Company, Morton Grove, Illinois

To all the children at Temple Israel.
Each and every one of you makes it feel like Hanukkah!—L.G.

For Ben and Chloe—you light up my life every day!—D.H.

Library of Congress Cataloging-in-Publication Data

Glaser, Linda.
Hoppy Hanukkah! / Linda Glaser ; illustrated by Daniel Howarth.
p. cm.
Summary: Two young bunnies learn about the customs of Hanukkah from their parents and grandparents before
they light the menorah, eat potato latkes, and play dreidel.
ISBN 978-0-8075-3378-9
[1. Hanukkah—Fiction. 2. Family life—Fiction. 3. Rabbits—Fiction.] I. Howarth, Daniel, ill. II. Title.
PZ7.G48047Ho 2009 [E]—dc22 2008055696

The design is by Carol Gildar.

For more information about Albert Whitman & Company, please visit our web site at www.albertwhitman.com.

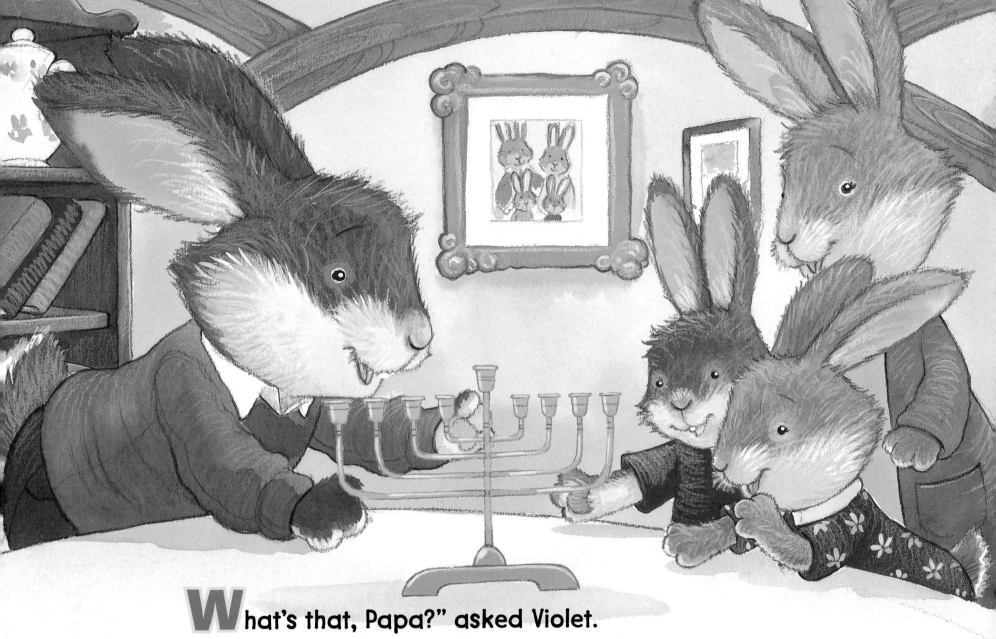

What's that, Papa?" asked Violet.

"Our menorah," said Papa. "Remember last year—when we lit the Hanukkah candles in it?"

"No. But let's do it again!" exclaimed Simon.

"We will," said Mama. "Hanukkah starts tonight.
Here, you can each put in one candle."

Violet and Simon each chose their favorite color.

"Now let's light them!" said Simon.
"Not yet," said Papa. "Not until the sun sets."

"I want Hanukkah *now!*" Violet hopped up and down on the couch.

"Me, too!" Simon hopped so hard his ears flopped.

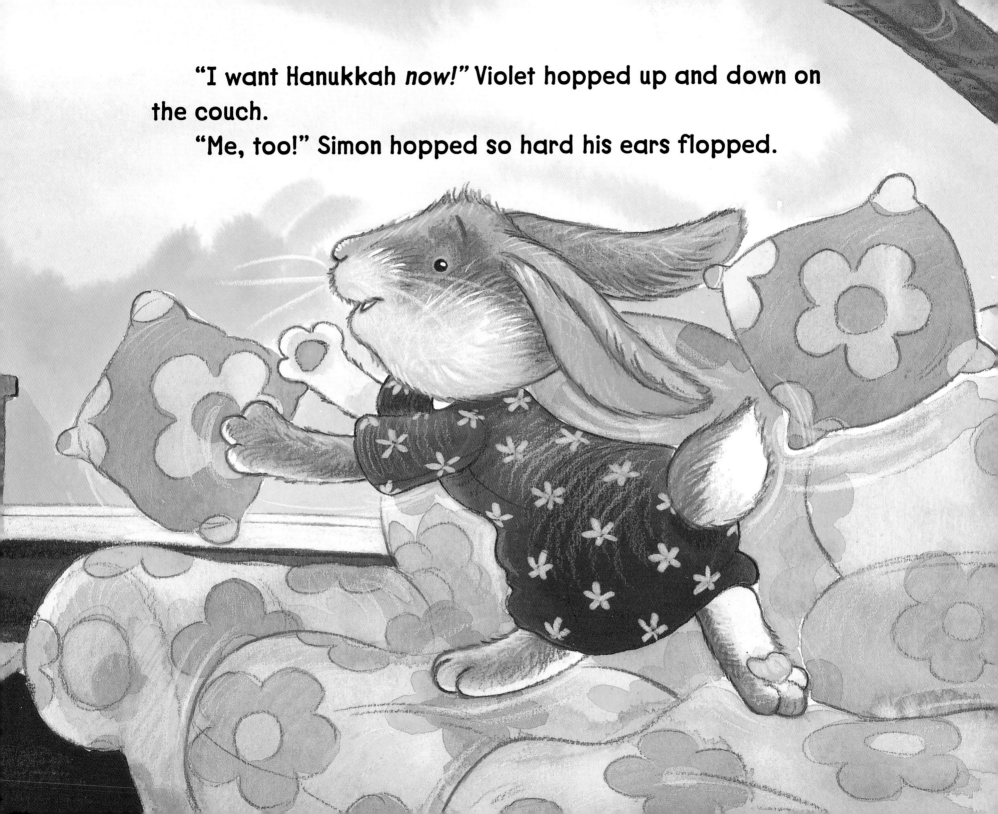

"We'll wait until nighttime," said Papa.

Mama nodded. "*That* makes it feel like Hanukkah. Each night we'll light one more candle—for eight nights."

Violet's eyes grew wide. "That sounds beautiful!"

"On the last night we'll fill the whole menorah." Papa beamed.

"Goody!" Violet clapped. "I'll make a wish and blow them all out. Like this."

"Me, too! Like this—" Simon blew so hard his ears flew!

Papa shook his head. "We don't blow them out. We put them in the window for everyone to see."

Mama nodded. "Jews have done this for a long, long time. *That* makes it feel like Hanukkah, too."

Violet's nose twitched. "What's Grandma cooking? It's the best smell ever."

"Potato latkes!" called Grandma. "Fried in oil for Hanukkah."

Grandpa patted his tummy. "Crispy latkes *always* make it feel like Hanukkah." Simon's nose wiggled so hard his tummy jiggled. "Let's eat!"

"Wait! Look!" Violet pointed. "The sun's going down."
"It's time!" cried Simon.

They hopped up and down—around the whole kitchen.
"Happy Hanukkah!" Grandma sang out.
Grandpa shook his head. "Around here, it's *Hoppy* Hanukkah!"

Giggling, Violet and Simon hopped
right to the table.
Papa said the blessings and lit
the candles. The whole room glowed.

"Now *this* feels like Hanukkah," said Mama.

Violet and Simon snuggled next to her.
They watched the candles burn . . .

and ate plenty of latkes.

Grandpa showed them how to play dreidel. What fun!

Grandma gave them each a Hanukkah present—ducky pajamas!

Mama tucked them into bed. "My little bunnies!
You know what *really* makes it feel like Hanukkah?"

They shook their heads. "What?"

She gave them each a soft squeeze. "YOU!"